One Hand, Two Hands

⁓

J·J
To

Cole
From

Date

Other Children's Books and Videos by Max Lucado

Just In Case You Ever Wonder

The Crippled Lamb

The Tallest of the Smalls

The Oak Inside the Acorn

Jacob's Gift

The Way Home:
A Princess Story

God's Great Big Love for Me

Tell Me the Story

Tell Me the Secrets

You Are Special

You Are Mine

If Only I Had a Green Nose

A Hat for Ivan

All You Ever Need

Coming Home

Best of All

Punchinello and the Most
Marvelous Gift

Lucia and the Razzly Dazzly
Wemberry Pies

Punchinello: One of a Kind

Hermie Books and Videos

Books:

Hermie: A Common
Caterpillar

Flo the Lyin' Fly

Webster the Scaredy Spider

The 12 Bugs of Christmas

Buzby the Misbehaving Bee

Hermie & Friends:
The Straight Path

Hermie & Friends:
The Race of Fear

A Fruitcake Christmas

Stanley the Stinkbug
Goes to Camp

To Share Or Nut To Share

Milo the Mantis Who
Wouldn't Pray

Hermie & Friends:
Buzby and the Grumble Bees

Videos

Hermie: A Common
Caterpillar

Flo the Lyin' Fly

Webster the Scaredy Spider

Buzby the Misbehaving Bee

A Fruitcake Christmas

Stanley the Stinkbug
Goes to Camp

Hermie and Wormie's Nutty
Adventure (previously titled
To Share Or Nut to Share)

Milo the Mantis
Who Wouldn't Pray

Buzby and the Grumble Bees

Hailey & Bailey's Silly Fight

Hermie & Friends Sing Along:
Hermie the Uncommon DJ

Hermie and the High Seas

Skeeter and the Mystery of
the Lost Mosquito Treasure

The Flo Show Creates a Buzz

Antonio Meets His Match

Max Lucado

One Hand, Two Hands

Oh, the ways we can help with our hands!

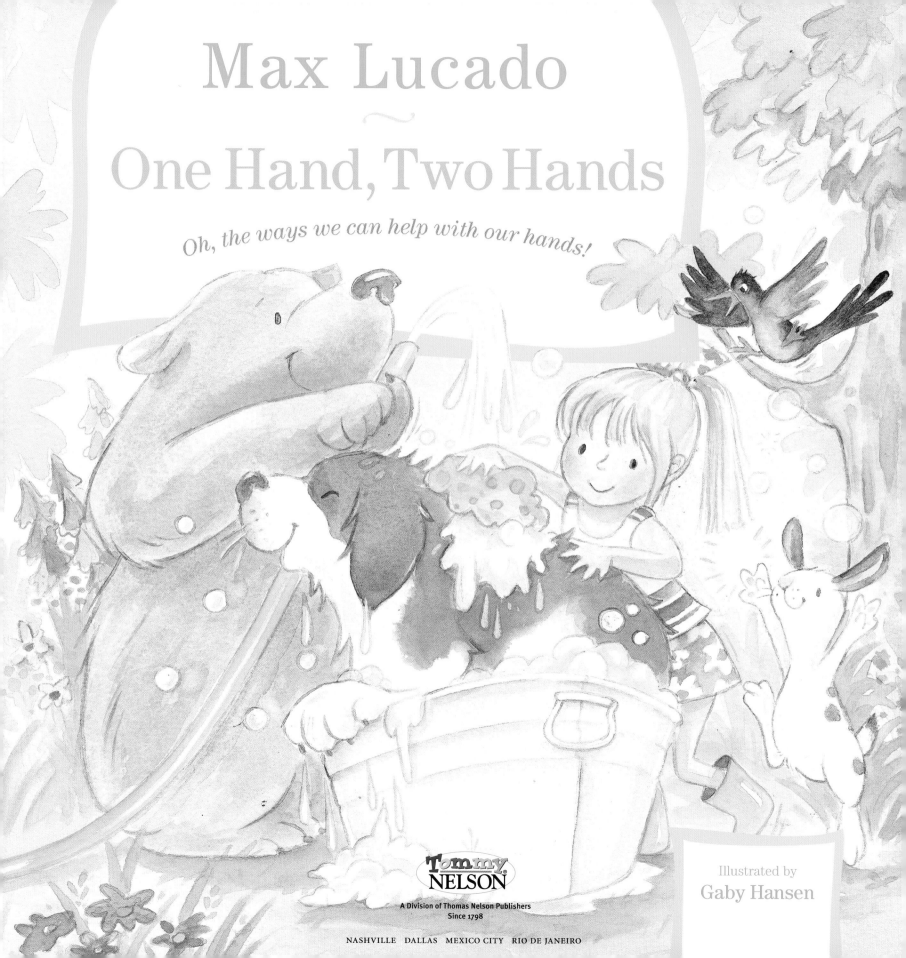

Tommy
NELSON

A Division of Thomas Nelson Publishers
Since 1798

NASHVILLE   DALLAS   MEXICO CITY   RIO DE JANEIRO

Illustrated by
Gaby Hansen

To Jacob and Greyson Lucado—
with deepest love

Published in Nashville, Tennessee, by Tommy Nelson®. Tommy Nelson is a registered trademark of Thomas Nelson, Inc.

Gaby Hansen, Illustrator

Karen Hill, executive editor to Max Lucado

Tommy Nelson® titles may be purchased in bulk for educational, business, fund-raising, or sales promotional use. For information, please e-mail SpecialMarkets@ThomasNelson.com.

Library of Congress Cataloging-in-Publication Data
Lucado, Max.
  One hand, two hands / by Max Lucado ; illustrations by Gaby Hansen.
    p. cm.
  Summary: Rhyming text explores some of the many things that one's hands can do, from petting a puppy and wiping a tear to folding in prayer.
  ISBN 978-1-4003-1649-6 (hardcover)
  [1. Stories in rhyme. 2. Hand—Fiction.] I. Hansen, Gaby, ill. II. Title.
  PZ8.3.L9615On 2010
  [E]—dc22
                          2010017787

Printed in Mexico

10 11 12 13 14 WC 6 5 4 3 2

Mfr.: Worldcolor / Queretero, Mexico / October 2010 / PPO # 114302

Dear Parent,

From first breath, your child began learning about hands. With cuddles, caresses, and comforting, you communicated your love. Your hands made your child feel secure and nourished.

And as your little one grew, there were more lessons about hands. What to touch. How to touch—"Gently," you said, as your child patted a puppy's tummy.

Your child knows that hands can be kind or harsh, helpful or hurtful. How? Because you've been teaching as your child has been growing. And your child knows that hands can help, too.

As you continue parenting and teaching, remind your little one that hands can help others in many ways. I hope this book comes in *hand-y!*

Max Lucado

One hand,
two hands,
five fingers,
ten.

Nails,
knuckles,
two thumbs,
and some skin . . .

For scratching,
latching, and petting a pup . . .

Combing and brushing
and **holding** a cup.

One right.
One left.
One here and
one there.

Clap 'em,
snap 'em,
wave 'em
in the air.

Squeeze them real tight and make your own fist.

Or flop 'em and bop 'em by bending your wrist.

In water they're wet.
In snow they feel cold.

Soap makes them clean
(at least, so I'm told).

Pick flowers, they smell sweet.
Squish cheese, they smell stinky.

Ooey. Pooey.
Right down to your pinky.

Button your shirt.
Tie your own shoe.

Play in the band!
Do-dee do-dee-do.

Dig in the dirt.
Draw lines in the sand.

Oh, the things we can do
because we have hands. . . .

Wipe tears. Give a gift.
Write Grandma a letter.

With hands and a hug,
we make people feel better.

Wash dishes with Mommy.
Put toys in the box.

Clean this and wipe that.
Even **pick up** our socks.

*With hands
we are helpers.
And at the
end of the day . . .

we fold them
together
and happily
pray:

"One hand, two hands, five fingers, ten . . .

"God, thanks for my hands. Please, use them again."

Helping Hands

My helping hands can . . .

- clean my room
- feed my pets
- set and clear the table
- gather the trash

Kind Hands

My hands are gentle and kind when I . . .

- draw a get-well card for a sick person
- carry a gift to my teacher
- put a Band-Aid on a friend's scraped knee
- share my snack

Loving Hands

My hands show love when I . . .

- ♥ fold them to pray
- ♥ clap for someone else
- ♥ wave to a friend
- ♥ hug my mom or dad

Think of ways your hands can be helping hands!